This book is dedicated

to everyone except Steve . . . Fuck Steve

A DAY TO CARE

BRAXTON HARRIS

A Day to Care
Copyright © 2022 by Braxton Harris

Tellwell Talent
www.tellwell.ca

ISBN
978-0-2288-8472-9 (Paperback)
978-0-2288-8473-6 (eBook)

The roads were bare on that October Tuesday morning. An eerie feeling hung in the air, something unexplainable. It was the feeling you get when something bad is about to happen. Some say it's a higher sense, others would blame it on angels. In the end, it didn't matter who or what it was blamed on; Frank Radcliffe never even noticed. He drove down the lonely road in his white Ford Bronco, too busy listening to Ed Robertson sing about what he would do if he had a million dollars. A smile stretched across his face as he thought about what he would do if he had a million of his own. He felt like he would be doing the same thing, or something similar.

After many years working in locations around the world, Frank had finally found a place he wanted to call home. Two years earlier while he was on the internet, he came across a job posting. It was something different, but it was something he thought he could be good at. He had been thinking about getting away, becoming a better person, living an honest lifestyle. This ad was more of a calling than an opportunity. He thought maybe he should answer it, so he did. They hired him almost immediately, without even conducting an interview. When he began, he was swift to impress the bosses. He later learned that they had been having some difficulty filling the position. At the time he was hired, all they were really looking for was for someone who could get the job done; if they could do the job well, even better. What Frank was doing went above and beyond, so when it came time for them to run his criminal record, they didn't mind looking the other way. That's how Frank ended up cooking for children at the daycare, and he hadn't had a bad day yet.

Bacon and pancakes were on the menu that morning, one of his favourite things to prepare. Not only because it was easy, but because they had the tendency to put the biggest and brightest smiles on the faces of the children. Many would come in sleepy and grumpy, feeling bitter about having to leave not only the comfort of their beds, but the comfort of their homes as well. Not to mention the feeling of abandonment when the moms and dads dropped them off and disappeared for the day. It was important for breakfast to be enjoyable; it was often an opportunity to distract them from being sad.

When Frank arrived, the building was almost empty. Kim was the only one there, as she most often was in the early morning. She was in charge of opening, and unless she was kidnapped, in jail or dead, she would be there.

"Good morning," Frank said as he entered. Kim was in the office which was the first room on the left upon entering. She poked out her head.

"Morning, Frank," she said sleepily as she tucked herself back inside, most likely pretending to work whilst waiting for the first child to arrive.

The rest of the daycare was open space. Dividers separated the room into sections, each decorated in its own theme and colour. Three washrooms were lined up against the back wall. They were designated for the children, and designed for them as well. So unless you were a child or a rainbow-riding leprechaun, you wouldn't be able to fit. There was a decent-sized staff room lined up against the wall after the office. A grown-up washroom was in there, along with a staff fridge, microwave and a dining table. A couch and coffee table were on the other side, along with two La-Z-Boy recliners and stacks of reading material.

Frank walked in the opposite direction of both of those room, to the back right corner where tiny tables and chairs had been set up. In the corner of that area was another door which led to the kitchen. Reaching with his hand, he felt along the wall until he found a switch. He flicked it on, and then there was light. He took in a deep breath through his nostrils. He loved the smell of kitchens, especially this kitchen. There was something about the combination of the equipment, seasonings, sauces and pilot lights that tickled his fancy. It was the way he wanted it; it was the way he maintained it. A hook on the wall held a clean apron next to the light switch. He took it down, slipping the neck strap over his head and tying the strings around his waist. He got out his favourite bowl and began collecting ingredients to mix inside. It wasn't long until the smell of bacon and pancakes began drifting through the building.

Parents had begun dropping off their little ones, some staying long enough to have a conversation with Kim, others leaving as quickly as they came. Audrey and Claire had shown up, both at seven o'clock. They worked as caretakers along with Kim. In the kitchen, Frank could hear the building filling up. Children had a way of being heard.

When the clock struck nine, forty-seven children were waiting not so patiently, as they sat around the dining tables. Frank was met with cheers when he carried in the breakfast tray. It held a large jug of orange juice and three insulated food containers. One was piled high with watermelon, another stacked into a mountain of pancakes, while the last one was filled past the brim with bacon. You had to be there to smell it.

Frank wasn't sure when Stacy had arrived, but she was there now. She had been giving the kids a lecture of some sort when he walked in. He hoped it wasn't on manners in regards to paying attention and respect to the person who was speaking.

"Good morning, Frank," Stacy glumly greeted him. She had lost the kids' attention and knew she wasn't getting it back.

"What's for bweakfast, Fwank?" Maverick asked. He was one of the vocally underdeveloped talkative toddlers. "It smells fucking awesome."

All the kids who knew better went silent when they heard what Maverick said; the ones who didn't went silent when Stacy spoke up.

"Maverick!" Stacy said in a loud, clear, stern voice. "We do not talk like that."

Maverick was startled by Stacy's reaction, and with the attention of the room on him, he began to tear up and cry. Stacy realized he didn't mean to say anything wrong. It was just a new word he had overheard somewhere and he thought that now would be a good time to use it.

"Maverick," Stacy lowered her tone, "that was a very bad word you said. You can't talk like that." She had approached him and was rubbing his back to calm him down. It seemed to have worked, because his sobs had now turned into sniffles.

"How come?" Maverick asked as he used his sleeve to wipe away the snot and tears from his face.

"Because bad people use bad words," Stacy said, "and you're not a bad guy."

The tension in the room eased up as the children began to rekindle previous conversations they had going on amongst each other. Frank had already set the tray on the serving table and was on his way back into the kitchen.

"What do we say to Frank?" Kim asked the children before he could get away.

"Thank you!" they shouted all at once, but not at the same time.

"You're all very welcome," Frank said with a smile. The shouting and screaming turned into slurping and chomping as Claire began handing out the plates that Audrey had portioned. Frank returned to the kitchen to begin his next task.

The rest of the morning went on as usual. When the kids were done eating, Frank went out to collect and clean the dishes. Once they were dry, he returned them to their rightful place on the shelves in the dining section. No one saw him go in, and no one saw him go out. This made it easy for him to slip back into the kitchen, which was where he needed to be.

He was making grilled cheese sandwiches today, and the kids sure knew how to gobble them up.

Retrieving his favourite frying pan, he placed it on the front right burner of the range and lit it up. Three clicks ticked before the flame lit. He turned it down, collected the rest of the ingredients and began grilling sandwiches, all while the children played. When it was time for lunch, Frank had it ready before the caretakers even had a chance to get the children gathered and settled. He left it all out on the table for them so they could eat whenever they were ready.

As soon as Frank returned to the kitchen, he could hear the children getting near. Cheers of joy erupted when the children discovered that grilled cheese sandwiches were being served. They were hungrier than Frank had expected, because the fifty sandwiches he made weren't even enough. He made another twenty when they asked for more, and still needed to make another seven after that. By the time lunch was over, the hungry and restless children were full and tired. It was the perfect condition to be in for a nap, which just so happened to be next on the agenda.

Across from the dining area, the caretakers had set out rows of mattresses with a series of colourful cartoon-riddled blankets. All of the children were lying down when Frank went in to collect the dishes, but not all of them were asleep. Stacy was in the office. He could hear her typing from where he was, even overtop of the gentle music echoing through the thrift-shop speakers. Audrey, Claire and Kim were all tending to the children who either couldn't or wouldn't go to sleep. Eventually they would get them down, as they always did, but it would take time. Frank was careful to be quiet as he picked up the empty dishes, returning them to the kitchen where he would get them cleaned up.

He plugged the sink and turned on the tap; the water began to rise as he gave a generous squirt of liquid dish detergent. Bubbles formed and the water swished and swirled as Frank dunked and scrubbed the dishes. Once they were clean, he placed them on a rack to dry. As he continued to clean, the slumbering silence was interrupted. A big bang echoed through the building, followed by shattering glass. Frank stopped what he was doing and listened. Slowly, he approached the door so he could peek out and see what had caused all the ruckus. But when he poked his head out, he was blindsided by terror.

Two masked men were in the building with guns drawn. Stacy, Claire, Audrey and Kim lay face down on the floor with their hands cuffed behind their backs. The children remained asleep as the men began collecting them in burlap sacks and dragging them away. As Frank looked on in horror, he was spotted by one of the masked men.

"Hey!" the man shouted. Frank swiftly slipped back into the kitchen. He could hear the men speaking to one another, but couldn't make out what was being said. Frank glanced toward the emergency exit at the back of the kitchen, but he never took it into consideration; he was too focused on the knives resting in the block on the counter beside it. Quickly he ran to grab the biggest one, then slid back toward the entrance. Tucking himself tight against the wall, he reached up and killed the lights.

The door cautiously opened, and the barrel of a gun slowly made its entrance. As one hand held on to the weapon, the other felt along the wall in search of the switch that controlled the lights. Frank waited patiently as the man struggled to locate it. Eventually, he found what he was looking for. He flipped the switch. Just as quickly as light filled the room, Frank swung out the knife, stabbing the man's hand and pinning him to the wall. He screamed in pain as he dropped the gun to remove the knife from his hand.

Frank rolled out from the wall, collecting the gun along the way as he stood up. He now had it pointed in the intruder's face.

"Unless you want a hole in your head, you had better stop moving," Frank said. The man did as he was told, leaving his hand stuck to the switch on the wall.

"What's going on in there?" the other man shouted from outside of the room.

"Tell him everything is fine." Frank spoke softly. The man didn't acquiesce. Instead, he decided to reach for the knife. But before he could get a grip on it, Frank turned the gun around and hammered the knife farther in with the butt of it. This time the knife made contact with the wrong wire. The man fried and sizzled as sparks flew, his body involuntarily performing a final dance before flopping to the floor. Frank turned the gun and aimed it toward the doorway. He knew the other man would be coming in soon, and when that happened, Frank was eager to squeeze the trigger.

The building had become engulfed in silence as both men waited to see what the other had planned. The silence didn't last long, due to the lack of patience from the second intruder.

"Is anyone alive in there?" the man shouted.

"Only one of us," Frank replied. The man could recognize that it wasn't his partner's voice.

"You shouldn't have done that," the man warned.

"I didn't," Frank replied. "He did it to himself, just like you're doing it to yourself." Frank held the gun steady, waiting for Intruder Number Two to step into his line of fire. Frank was waiting for something that was never going to happen. Instead, he heard the drop of a pin, and then a grenade rolled in.

Thinking as quickly as possible, Frank ran to the refrigerator, swung open the door and tucked himself in as best he could. It wasn't a good fit, but it was a fit. The grenade blew up. It wasn't as big of an explosion as he was expecting, but it was big enough for him to not be able to remember it. The destruction was contained to the kitchen. The walls were damaged, but intact. Everything else in the room was demolished.

Everything except Frank's will to live, his love for the children and his desire for revenge.

Frank woke up from a darkness he couldn't remember. Clueless to the world, the only thing that he fully understood was that he was a person. Machines beeped and whooshed as they pumped and drained, working in unison to keep him alive. As he began to regain consciousness, he understood that he was in a hospital. Many greeting cards were set across the desk beneath the window, darkness beyond that. He opened his mouth to speak, unsure of what he was going to say, or to whom he was going to say it. Whichever the case, it didn't matter. His throat was so dry that his attempt to speak threw him into a coughing fit. He needed something to drink. He scanned the room once again, this time looking for a glass of water. There was none. He continued to cough. Taking in some deep, controlled breaths, he was able to make it go away. Yet he was still left with a tickle in his throat. He tried to clear it, which only brought back more coughing. At some point the disturbance was enough to garner the attention of one of the nurses.

A young redheaded lady poked her head in. When she saw Frank, her jaw dropped.

"Oh my goodness!" she exclaimed with genuine surprise. "This is . . . hold on. I'll be back." She was gone out the door before Frank had the chance to ask for some water. It didn't matter, though; she wasn't gone long. She came back with a clipboard and another nurse, this one carrying a cup in her hands. She handed it to Frank as he reached out to accept it, and drank it all up before he could even taste what it was. The cool liquid rushing down his throat provided some very much needed relief. He took in some deep breaths and relaxed. The redheaded nurse had been checking the machines and writing notes on the clipboard.

"You must have been thirsty," the second nurse said as she took the cup back from him.

"Not thirsty, just dry," Frank replied.

"Do you want me to get you some more?"

"No thanks, I'm fine for now," Frank said. "I'm more interested in finding out what's going on."

"Yes, that makes sense. I'm Sarah, and I'm one of the head night nurses here at the Glendondale hospital. The nurse checking your vitals is Briar. She's the one who has been taking care of you the most over the last three weeks."

"Three weeks?" Frank asked.

"Yes," said Sarah, "it's been a little scary."

"I don't understand why I'm here."

"You must not remember a thing."

"No, not much," Frank said, "but I kind of feel like things are slowly starting to coming back."

"Well, I can tell you what we know," Sarah continued. "You were involved in an explosion, that's why you're here."

Frank thought for a moment. When she said "explosion," it triggered something in his memory. But it was something he couldn't quite remember. Frank looked over at Briar who had been monitoring the machines. She had been writing notes on her clipboard, carrying an expression on her face of someone who had been witness to a miracle. She brought the clipboard over to Sarah and showed her something.

"Unbelievable," she whispered to herself.

"You think you're mind-blown now, wait till you see the other charts," Briar said as she went back to tending the machines.

"So what's my situation?" Frank asked Sarah.

"Your situation is, you have no situation. Not health wise, anyway."

"What does that mean?"

"Yesterday we began to search for a next of kin. A decision needed to get made soon, very soon." Sarah's words held shame.

"What kind of decision?" Frank asked, with a general idea of the decision she was speaking of.

"I feel like you know," she said, "and I feel like my recommendation would have been to shut it down."

"Shut it down?" Frank asked. "You mean pull the plug?"

"Frank, no one was expecting you to live. You were far too damaged."

"What happened?" he asked.

"I don't know," Sarah said. "But according to these charts you're making an incredible recovery."

"I'm still not entirely grasping the situation."

"It's a doozy, Frank. Maybe it would even be best for you to not remember."

"What don't you want to tell me?"

"It doesn't matter whether I want to do it or not. The plain and simple fact is that I'm not allowed to tell you," Sarah explained.

"Says who?" Frank asked.

"Well, there are some cops who say so, and I'm not one to cross them."

"I don't see why I can't know."

"Because they want to talk to you. They need to talk to you first in order to properly conduct their investigation."

"When can I see them?"

"They're on their way right now. I got one of the other night nurses to call them when Briar came and told us you were up."

"When will they get here?" Frank asked.

"Oh, I'm not too sure about that." She thought for a moment. "I imagine they're at home in bed at this hour. With that being said, I don't think it'll take them long to be on their way. They just need to throw on some clothes. If they're tired enough they might grab a coffee on the way. I can't see it being more than a half hour."

"Okay." Frank had no more questions.

"I'm going to let you rest up," she said, then turned to Briar who was still observing the monitors. "How are things over there?"

"It's . . . it's phenomenal," Briar said. "According to this he's almost half way to a full recovery."

"That can't be right." Sarah approached Briar to examine the monitors for herself. She looked on in disbelief. Frank couldn't see what they were looking at, and wouldn't have been able to tell you what it meant if he could. He was feeling good, though, and as the minutes ticked along, he could feel himself getting better. Sarah looked back at Frank and wondered if the man she was looking at was even human. "Make sure you find him something to eat. It's a long time till breakfast, and I think he's going to need some energy."

"Yes, ma'am," Briar replied. Sarah walked out and away. They listened to the sound of her footsteps drift off into the distance.

"You're famous." Briar broke the silence. "You don't know it, maybe you don't believe it, but it's true. You're all over the news. People were praying for you. People were praying for you and God listened."

"I don't understand," Frank said.

"That's what all those cards are for." Briar motioned toward the greeting cards on the desk under the window. "People have been dropping them off for you. Complete strangers even."

"Why?"

"Because of the story they ran on the news."

"What was the story?"

"It was about—" Briar realized she was telling him something she shouldn't be speaking about. This was supposed to be left to the detectives. She knew better, she had just let her excitement get the best of her. "I don't think I should be talking about it. I don't want to get into any trouble." Frank didn't want her to get in trouble either. He especially didn't want to be the one to get her in trouble, so he didn't press her any further. "Are you feeling hungry?" she asked.

"I could eat a whole horse," Frank said.

"I don't think we have any horse here, but I'm sure I could find you some sandwiches."

"That would be great." Frank was grateful.

"I'll be back," she said and left the room, leaving Frank once again listening to fading footsteps. He closed his eyes and relaxed, but didn't go to sleep. He had done enough of that for a while. He took in a deep breath, held it a moment and let it out. His memory was beginning to catch up: he knew who he was and what he did for work. He just couldn't remember what had happened to land him in the hospital. He wasn't worried; he was sure he would remember eventually. He opened his eyes so he could look over and see the cards on the desk. He appreciated the gesture, but he didn't understand it. As he tried to read what he could from where he was sitting, he could hear the return of footsteps. Whoever it was, was moving fast, as if they were excited. A quick three knocks were rapped on the open door. Sarah didn't wait for a response before entering.

"Right this way, gentlemen," Sarah said toward the door.

Two tired-looking men walked in. Neither of them appeared to have taken the time to shave, as stubble littered their chins beneath their moustaches. They were dressed in what business people would wear on Casual Friday. Khaki jeans and a red wrinkled polo shirt for one of the men; the other man had a tropical design on his sea-blue button-up shirt. The top three buttons were open, revealing a white V-neck undershirt with curly brown hairs poking out of it. He had on faded blue jeans with cowboy boots tucked inside. If it weren't for the colour, their moustaches would have been identical. The man in the khakis had a blond one, while the man in the blue jeans' was black. They chewed gum simultaneously as they walked in with an aura of confidence. Their faces revealed no expression. Frank began to wonder if he had done something wrong and was in trouble, but then he remembered the cards lined up on the desk. He didn't think strangers would show that much love for someone who had done something wrong. His mind was eased, but still he worried.

"Frank, these are the officers who wanted to speak with you," Sarah said. "I'm going to leave you here with them, but Briar is going to stay to watch the monitors. A recovery like this has never been seen before. We must keep watch." She walked away before there was time to say goodbye. Frank turned his attention to the men.

"Hello, Frank," the man wearing the khakis said. "I'm Lieutenant Daniels. This here's my partner, Lieutenant Richinski. I understand you've been made aware that we are lieutenants of the law."

"Yes, I have," Frank replied.

"Good," Daniels said. "So how are you feeling?"

"I've been better."

"Haven't we all?" Daniels asked rhetorically, as he took a moment to collect his thoughts. "Listen, I'm just going to cut to the chase. We were hoping we could ask you a few questions about what happened, if you don't mind."

"I can tell you what I know, but I gotta warn you, there's not much I remember," Frank said.

"Yeah, that's all right." Daniels continued, "I was thinking that maybe if we talk for a little while, something could jog your memory."

"I hope so," Frank said. The man who was introduced as Richinski pulled out a pen and notepad he had tucked into one of his pockets. With a flick of the wrist, he flipped open the notepad and clicked the pen, popping out the tip.

"Am I in any trouble?" Frank asked.

Daniels chuckled and looked over at Richinski, who was doing the same.

"Trouble?" It was Richinski speaking now. "Are you kidding me? You're a hero, man."

"How?" Frank wondered.

"What's the last thing you remember?" Daniels asked. Frank did some more thinking, as he had been doing ever since he awoke. Memories were fading in fast, but nothing in regards to how he ended up in the hospital.

"The last thing I remember," Frank said, breaking the moment's silence, "I remember going to work . . . I remember getting to work. Kim was there, and then I started making pancakes." Frank paused and thought a bit more. "That all, that's it. I can't remember anything else." Richinski had been writing notes while Frank was speaking.

"Nothing else?" Daniels pressed.

"Not so far," Frank replied. "So, now what can you tell me?"

"Well, Frank"—it was Daniels—"there's no easy way to say this, but the kids are gone."

"What do you mean gone?"

"They've been kidnapped," Daniels said, "along with the staff, obviously other than you."

"All of them?" Frank asked.

"All the ones working that day," Daniels replied.

"Why was I spared?" Frank's question made Daniels chuckle. It was funny to him in a strange way.

"Spared?" Daniels questioned Frank. "I wouldn't go as far as calling it 'spared.' It was more of a left-for-dead type of situation." Frank experienced a moment of déjà vu; he tried to hold on to it, but it slipped away. At that moment he knew the memory was there, and he would eventually be able to get it back.

"How was I discovered?"

"You were in the kitchen. Looked like you crawled into the fridge when a live grenade was thrown in and blew up," Daniels told him.

"Were there any dead men?" Frank asked. "I'm remembering something . . . I remember a man dying, a man getting shocked." Frank thought a moment longer before he lit up with excitement. "A man. Getting . . . getting electrocuted . . . by the light switch." Daniels and Richinski shared a moment of eye contact, confirming to each other that they were hearing things correctly.

"There were no bodies or signs of anyone anywhere. You were all that remained. Even the camera footage is kaput."

"How?" Frank asked.

"We have no idea," Daniels said. "We're stumped, we don't have any leads. No bodies were found. However, we did discover some damage to the light switch in the kitchen. It looked like someone had stabbed it."

"What does that mean?"

"It means there was a struggle, and that you put up a fight," said Daniels.

"How did you conclude that?" Frank asked.

"The light switch, with the knife damage." Daniels carried on, "We discovered bits of burnt flesh around it. We ran some DNA tests on it, to see if we could get a match. It wasn't a match to you or to anyone else we have in our system."

"So someone was electrocuted?"

"Yes, we can confirm that, but we can't confirm that anyone died and we don't think that happened either."

"Why not?"

"Because why would they take the body with them? Why wouldn't they just leave it to burn with you?"

"Maybe it was the body of someone who could link you to whoever else is responsible."

"That could be," Daniels said, "but we don't think so."

Silence once again filled the room as both sides took in the new information. Frank looked over toward the window, and then down to the desk.

"I don't understand the cards," Frank said.

"What cards?" Daniels asked.

"The cards on the desk, the cards from the people. Why am I being hailed as a hero? It doesn't seem like I did anything."

"You did, though. You fought back, and you gave up your life doing it, or so you thought you were."

"I don't deserve them," Frank said. "I'm not a hero—I didn't do a darn thing."

"Listen, Frank. I got a pretty good feeling about you, and I think it's only a matter of time before your memory comes back completely. You'll be able to give us the information we need to find these kids. That sounds pretty heroic to me," Daniels said in an attempt to make Frank feel better about himself. It didn't work.

"I think we got as much as we can for now." Daniels was speaking to Richinski. "Maybe we oughta let him rest up a bit. We could probably use some rest ourselves." Richinski nodded his head in agreement.

"All right." Daniels turned his attention back to Frank. "You try to rest up. If you remember anything, feel free to give us a call," he said while handing Frank two business cards. "Anytime of day, anytime of night, you understand?"

"Yeah," Frank said, as he accepted and examined what Daniels handed to him. One read Lieutenant Daniels, the other Lieutenant Richinski. Each had their personal contact information, and they both had matching numbers that went to the police station.

"We're gonna find those kids," Daniels assured him, then turned to Richinski. "Let's get outta here." Richinski gave Frank a wave and exited the room, with Daniels close behind.

Frank lay in silence for a moment, once again listening to the machines. Briar was watching him and noticed the troubled look on his face.

"You are a hero," Briar spoke softly, in hopes of raising his spirits.

"I can see why you would think that," Frank replied.

"And I can see why I believe it," she said. "Frank, you literally put your life on the line for those kids, and nearly lost in the process."

"But I lost the kids, didn't I?" Frank was getting upset. "A hero wouldn't have done that—a hero would have rescued them. Anyone can stand up and die."

"But not everyone has the heart to do it," Briar was quick to respond. Frank looked at her and thought long about it.

"I don't deserve those cards," he said.

"If they're bothering you that much, I can get rid of them." Briar was trying her best to keep him comfortable.

"No," Frank said, "don't do that. I think I'm gonna need them."

"For what?" Briar was curious.

"Motivation."

"By the looks of things"—Briar held up Frank's charts—"you've been plenty motivated already."

"That's fine, but I'm not talking about my health."

"Well then, what is it you're looking to find motivation for?" she asked.

"To earn them," Frank answered, but Briar didn't understand and became confused.

"What do you mean?" she asked.

"The people gave me those cards under the impression that I'm someone who I am not," Frank said. "So now, I'm going to get out there and be the someone I was supposed to be, the someone I should have been. I got the cards, but I didn't earn them, not by a long shot. So that's what I'm going to get out there and do."

"Oh." Briar was beginning to understand. "But how do you plan on doing that?"

"I'm going to find the kids," Frank stated, "and then I'm going to get them back."

Frank swung his legs off the bed and began pulling out the tubes and needles plugged into him.

"Frank, you can't do that," Briar said as she stepped forward to stop him. He gently pushed her aside.

"You have no legal grounds to keep me here," Frank announced. Briar stepped back; she knew he was right. "Where are my clothes?" he asked. Briar walked to the cabinet stationed in the corner by the desk. Opening it up, she reached in and retrieved some hospital-issued clothing.

"The clothes you came in with couldn't be saved," Briar said as she passed him his new attire. Frank inspected the navy blue sweatsuit. It looked and felt like it would be comfortable. Even if it wasn't, it didn't matter; it was going to have to do.

"Did I have any belongings? My keys or my wallet?" Frank asked.

"Just a moment," Briar said and left the room.

Frank took the time to change into the new outfit he was given. It was comfortable and fit fairly fine. He was worried that Briar might tell Sarah or some of the other night nurses that he was planning on leaving. He was certain they couldn't stop him, but he was concerned about getting slowed down. He didn't want to spend the time it would take to argue, when there were so many tiny lives on the line. However, it was a concern he didn't need to worry about; Briar came back unattended. In her hands were some black-and-white runners, along with a clear plastic bag that contained a set of keys. Frank recognized the keys as his own, but the shoes he had never seen before.

"These keys were all you had on you," she said as she handed him the bag with the keys. "You didn't have any shoes, so I got these from the back. They're the new ones they got for our staff." Frank looked at the shoes in her hands, then the ones on her feet.

"Are they comfortable?" Frank asked.

"Like walking on clouds of sunshine," Briar replied.

"Thank you," Frank said, as he accepted the gift. He gave them a quick but thorough examination. He was impressed. Kneeling down, he slid them on and tied them up. When he stood, he got a clearer understanding of Briar's love for the shoes.

"They're nice" was all he could think to say.

"You don't have to tell me." She was on her way to the closet in the corner next to the desk. She opened it up, pulled out a large empty garbage bag and handed it to him.

"What's this for?" he asked.

"To pack your motivation." She gestured toward the desk holding the cards. Frank walked over and collected them into the bag. When he turned around, she was standing by the door holding two more bags: these ones were full. Even though he couldn't see through the plastic, Frank knew what was inside. He asked her anyway.

"What are those?"

"These are the rest of them."

Frank Radcliffe stepped out of the Glendondale hospital a physically healed man. It was early morning and the sun hadn't even thought about rising yet, as Frank slung his bags over his shoulder to begin his quest home. Parked along the edge of the sidewalk were a couple of taxi cabs. There was a box in Frank's closet at home. Inside was cash designated for use on a rainy day. He didn't need a weatherman to tell him it was a good day to use it.

He approached one of the cabs and explained his situation. Due to the fact that Frank didn't have any money to pay up front, and that the cabbie had been burned too many times before, he refused to give him a lift. Frank figured he would be stuck walking, but decided to try and ask the next cab anyway. That cabbie was all right with it and agreed to take him home. Frank opened the back door, stuffed his bags in, pushed them over and sat inside. Frank told him his address, and before long they were pulling up in front of Frank's house. He looked at his empty driveway and wondered where his Ford Bronco might be. Considering the last place he had it was at the daycare, he thought maybe he should check there.

"Can you give me a minute?" Frank requested. "I'll run in and grab the money, but I gotta get you to take me somewhere else after."

"If you got the money, I got the time," the cabbie said gleefully. Frank was pleased. Opening the door, he stepped out. He took out the bags of cards and dragged them into the house with him. Once inside, he noted that everything appeared to be just as he left it, or how he remembered it being when he left. He was quick to get to the box of money in the closet, but he was quicker to get to the box behind it. In that box there was something he wasn't ready to give up when he left his past life. Something in the back of his mind always told him to hold on to it. It could help with the rain, as well. He opened it up to reveal a pistol with a few rounds of ammunition. He checked to make sure it was loaded. When he saw that it was, he tucked it into his waistline at the back of his pants. He pulled his sweater down over top to conceal it. He put both of the boxes back after he had retrieved his gun and stuffed his pockets with a couple fistfuls of cash.

Outside, the cabbie had been working on a newspaper crossword puzzle while the meter ran. The back door opened and Frank slipped in.

"I need to go to Fifty-first Avenue and Seventeenth Street," Frank said.

"You mind if we square up first?" the driver asked.

"Not at all." Frank reached into his pocket, pulling out enough cash to cover the ride and then some. The cabbie counted it as soon as it was handed over. When he thought he had made a mistake and counted too high, he started over and counted again. He ended up with the same result and was satisfied. They drove away, flitting between the streetlights and the darkness.

Thirteen minutes later, the cab pulled in to the daycare parking lot. At the far end of the lot was a white Ford Bronco. Frank smiled as they parked next to it.

"How much do I owe you?" asked Frank.

"Are you kidding me?" the cabbie asked in return. "You already gave me way more than enough, man. I can go knock up a broad right now and not have to worry about saving money for my college fund." He was making a slight exaggeration.

"Thanks for helping me out, man," Frank said.

"No problem," the driver replied.

As Frank was stepping out, the cabbie shouted, "Hey!" Frank stopped and listened.

"You ever need to get anywhere again, feel free to call me." The cabbie handed him his business card.

"Thanks, but it shouldn't be necessary," said Frank.

"Why not?" the cabbie asked, retracting his offered card. "You don't like my driving or something?"

"That's not it. Your driving was just fine," Frank told him. "But do you see this Bronco I asked you to park beside?" Frank pointed to the vehicle.

"Yeah, I see it."

"It's mine," Frank said as he shut the door before the cabbie had a chance to respond. He approached his beloved Bronco, while the cab backed out and drove away. Frank was left alone in the darkness of the dawn.

He stood in silence for a moment longer to soak in the moment. It was the last breath of peace he was going to get for a while; he could feel it. Frank pushed the Unlock button on his key fob. The locks popped up and he stepped toward the driver's-side door. He was reaching for the handle when he stopped and thought otherwise. He wanted to see what the daycare looked like on the inside. He wanted to see the damage, and maybe if he was lucky, he would see something capable of reviving his memory. He had a key to the place; it hung on the same fob as the keys to his house and his Bronco. It was given to him because he would often go in early, especially when there was baking to be done. He unlocked the door and stepped inside. A continuous beep began to emit from the security panel. He had thirty seconds to shut it off before security would be alerted and he'd be dealing with the cops. He walked over, typed in the code and pressed Enter.

The beeping stopped.

He flicked the light switch, which was right next to the panel. The room lit up. At first glance, there didn't appear to be very much damage at all. Toys remained scattered across the floor; nothing had been put away since the day of the incident. He walked through the rest of the room at a casual pace, scanning for clues and digging for memory. Nothing had come up by the time he reached the dining area. The door to the kitchen wasn't where it was supposed to be. Instead of being in its proper position, it was lying on the floor in bits and pieces. He could see plenty of damage along the wall. He walked to where the door once was and entered what was left of the kitchen.

Frank imagined it would look bad in there, but he didn't imagine it to be as bad as it was. After observing the damage, he couldn't understand how or why he was alive. Nothing in that room had survived. He walked farther along, examining the area, beginning to reminisce. It was sad; he'd had many great days working in that place. He understood he was most likely standing in there for the last time. It was quiet without the kids. As he took his trip down memory lane, he heard their playful laughter, but it was only in his mind. He let his mind drift completely to enjoy the memories of how the place used to be. That's why he didn't hear the front door open, why he didn't hear someone come in.

When he brought himself back to reality, he knew it was time to leave. He collected his thoughts and headed toward where the door used to be. He had one foot out the kitchen, when the barrel of a pistol was pressed tight to the side of his head. Frank was quick to slip back as the assailant pulled the trigger, firing the gun and hitting nothing but wall. He was able to take hold of his attacker's arm after the shot and wrestle the gun out of their grasp. It fell to the floor. While holding their arm tight, Frank flipped himself around, positioning himself so the intruder was behind him. Jumping into the air, he released their arm while delivering a vicious donkey kick, sending them across the room into a pile of broken toys and dirty diapers.

"Frank, stop!" a woman shouted from the floor. Frank recognized her voice and knew immediately that he had made a mistake.

"Patricia!" Frank shouted in shock as he ran toward her. "I'm so sorry." Frank knelt down and helped her up. Patricia was the boss of the bosses. She owned and had a hand in operating the daycare. She had trained the management team well enough to handle the day-to-day business on their own. Over time, they had seen less and less of her. That's why she wasn't there on the day of the abduction.

"What are you doing here?" Patricia asked

"I came to pick up my Bronco," Frank explained, "but when I got here, I wanted to see what it looked like inside. I wanted to see what was left."

"Without the kids, it doesn't matter what's left."

"What are you doing here?" Frank now asked.

"I got an alert on my phone when the alarm was disarmed. I didn't realize you were out of the hospital; I didn't even know you woke up. I thought you were an intruder . . . I thought you were one of them, that maybe they came back."

"And no one knows who they are?"

"Not so much as a clue," Patricia said as she pulled out a cigarette from her purse and lit up.

"Why are you smoking in here?"

"Why does it matter? It's over. It's all over anyway." She took a drag and blew the smoke into the air.

"So that's it?" Frank asked. "You're just giving up?"

"Fuck you, Frank," she snapped. "You don't know what it's like—you don't know how it is to lose it all."

"You don't think I know what it's like?" Frank's voice carried a hint of fury. "I know darn well what it's like."

"Yeah, and how the hell would you know?"

"Because I lost them, too." Frank spoke more softly now. Patricia felt Frank's pain and understood. She dropped the cigarette and crushed it with her foot. Frank looked down and recognized her runners. They were similar to the ones he was wearing.

"I'm running away," Patricia announced.

"Well, you got on the right shoes for it," Frank said. "But what are you running away from?"

"From everything. I'm changing my name and going very far away. Very, very far away. I'm even going under the knife, Frank. I'll have a whole new look when I'm done."

"I don't understand."

"The children were taken away under my watch. They were my responsibility at the time, and I lost them. I lost them all, every single one of them."

"That's not what it's like," Frank argued, but Patricia was quick to snap back.

"It is what it's like, because that's what happened!" she shouted. "You can sugar-coat it any damn way you please, but when it boils down to the truth, I'm gonna be the one caught standing with my pants down."

"You're a victim here, Patricia," said Frank. "I mean, this could have happened to anyone."

"Well, it didn't happen to anyone," Patricia barked at him. "It happened to me!" When she realized that her anger was getting the best of her, she stopped talking and took some deep breaths to relax. Once she was in control of herself, she continued, but with a lowered voice. "I'm getting sued."

"By who?"

"By all of them, all the parents. Forty-eight cases against me."

"Why forty-eight? Who else is suing you?"

"Because Clayton's parents are divorced, they're suing me separately." Patricia paused. "On top of that, the business is shut down, with no plans to reopen and no money coming in."

"You can fix it," Frank said. This made Patricia giggle.

"Don't be silly, Frank. I can't fix it, and even if I could, who would ever trust me with their kids again? My reputation is ruined."

"You think I'm being silly?" Frank asked. "How silly are you going to feel when you find out you can't afford to run away?"

"Oh, I can afford it, Frank. I have plenty in my savings, and with the employees missing, well, I guess I don't have to pay them."

Frank looked at her with disgust and disappointment. "I didn't think you were like that," he said

"Well then, maybe you shouldn't think," she retorted. After the words were out, she thought otherwise. "Sorry, Frank. I didn't mean to talk to you like that. Listen, since you're here, I'll write you a cheque for what I owe you. I'll even put a little cherry on top since it'll be the last one, to show you how much your work was appreciated. It'll be a nice one."

With that, she left, heading toward the front of the building where the office was. As she walked away, Frank used his time to further examine the place. He casually strolled around where the children once made crafts and played games, where they screamed for attention and cried for their parents, where they ate healthy meals and smiled with missing teeth. As he paced and reminisced, something odd took hold of his attention in his peripheral vision. It was small, it was miniscule, it appeared to be irrelevant. He could see how the police could have missed it. Having not been at the daycare on a regular basis, they would have no idea that it didn't belong. He walked over, knelt down and gently picked it up with his fingers. In his hand was a feather from what appeared to be a chicken. Patricia stepped out of the office and approached him with a cheque in her hand.

"Here, Frank," she said as she held it out to him whilst making her approach. "I think it's time for both of us to lea—" Patricia stopped talking and looked at what Frank was holding. "What is that?" she asked.

"Isn't it obvious?" Frank said. "It's a chicken feather."

"Where did you find it?"

"Down here in the corner. I'm thinking it must've fallen off of one of the intruders. None of the children come from any farms."

"How did the cops miss it?"

"I don't know," Frank said, "but I had better go give them a call." Frank began to leave when Patricia stopped him.

"Hold on, Frank," she said. "I don't think that's such a good idea."

"What do you mean? Don't you want to get the kids back?"

"Yeah, but can we really trust them?"

"Trust who?"

"The cops—we can't trust them. Maybe they can help us find the kids, but the way they missed this piece of evidence makes me question whether or not they're capable. On top of that, what kind of justice will they really bring? The law always protects the scumbags. They never deliver any real justice, the justice they deserve."

"What kind of justice are we talking about?"

"You know damn well what kind of justice, Frank," Patricia said.

"You think we should kill them?" Frank asked.

"If you can find them," she said, as Frank looked down at the feather in his hand.

"Oh, I can find them," he assured her. "I can find anyone."

"I know you can." Patricia paused. "And you will, Frank, so when you do, I want you to kill them. I want you to kill them all." She handed Frank his cheque and walked away. Frank folded it up and tucked it into his pocket, bringing his full attention back to the feather.

"I got you," Frank whispered to himself. "I got you now, you jive turkey. Next I just gotta figure out who you are."

Moments later Frank was exiting the building. When he stepped outside, there was no sign that Patricia had ever even been there. The Bronco was once again all alone in the fading darkness. He climbed inside and fired it up. The Bronco rumbled with power, and Frank rumbled with rage. He backed out of the parking stall and drove out. The sun was finally beginning to rise; it was destined to be a busy day.

The Chicken Shack on 49th Street and 44th Avenue was a popular place for lunch and supper, but anytime before or in between was as dead as the birds they served. Which was why the staff found it odd to see a white Ford Bronco parked in the lot when they got there to start their morning shift. They could see a man was inside, but no one could see who he was, as he had the seat leaned back with a hat worn low on his head. Most of the staff found it to be humorous and began making fun of him in regards to his health and dedication to his eating habits.

Michelle wasn't a fan of the jokes. The Bronco and the man inside scared her. She was incredibly nervous. Something didn't seem right about it. She wanted to speak with Ted, the manager, but he wasn't scheduled to be in until noon. It was currently 10:45 and the Bronco had been there since who knew when.

She wanted to call the cops but didn't know what for; he wasn't doing anything illegal. She knew something was going to happen—she could feel it in the air—but there was no way of getting any help until what was destined to happen, happened. She had Ted's number saved on her phone. After giving it some very serious thought and consideration, she decided to give him a call. Stepping away from her duties, she went to the back, where there was a room that provided her with some privacy. She took her phone out of her pocket and began scrolling through her contacts. When she found Ted she called him.

The phone rang twice before he picked up.

"Hello," he greeted cheerfully.

"Hi. Um, it's Michelle."

"Hi, Michelle. What's going on?" Ted asked.

"Well, it's not really something that's going on, it's more of something that I think is going to go on."

"Is everything all right?"

"Yes, for now," Michelle said. "There's a man sitting out in the parking lot, waiting for us to open, I think. But he doesn't look right. I can sense something is wrong. I don't like the feeling I have about this."

"What is he doing?" Ted asked

"Nothing," she replied. "Just sitting there, watching, waiting."

"Well, I know I'm not there to fully grasp the dynamics of the situation. But I feel like I can assure you that everything is going to be fine."

"I wish I could be comfortable with that." Michelle spoke with honesty.

"I mean, I'm sure they would be able to manage without you. How would you feel if we let you go home for the day?"

"I would appreciate that," Michelle responded. "And it is a very kind gesture. But aside from the fact that I need the hours, I'm simply too afraid to go out there. If I were to leave, I would have to walk right past his Bronco."

"Wait a minute . . ." Ted sounded stunned. "Did you just say a Bronco?"

"Yeah, he's out there sitting in it."

"Is it white?" he asked. Ted's heart sank in his chest before she could tell him the answer that he already knew.

"Yeah," she said, "how did you know?"

"Who's the supervisor on shift right now?" Ted asked sharply, the joy stripped from his voice and replaced with panic.

"It's Dylan," she replied. "What's going on?" But she would get no response; Ted had hung up.

Michelle went back to the front of the store where everyone was gathered tending to their morning duties. She wanted to talk to Dylan, but when she found him, he was already on the phone, talking to someone else. She had a pretty good feeling about who it was. Dylan looked toward Michelle: major concern was plastered on his face. She couldn't hear what he was saying, but she could tell he was taking directions. The phone was cradled between his ear and shoulder. A notepad was open in one hand, while a pen was taking notes with the other. Dylan was obedient when it came to the bosses; that's why he had the position that he did. He hung up the phone and cleared his throat. This caught the attention of most staff—the ones who didn't hear him were quick to listen when he began to speak.

"Hey, guys, I need you to listen up for a minute," Dylan said. Everyone stopped what they were doing and waited to hear what he had to say. "So I just got off the phone with Ted, and I've been given orders to not open the store." This was met with cheers.

"Does that mean we get to go home?" Jerry asked. Jerry was seventeen, working on his final year of high school. This was a part-time job he'd acquired to help pay for video games and energy drinks. The job wasn't important; he didn't mind the idea of a day off.

"No," Dylan replied, "he's on his way in right now. He'll be able to answer any of your questions."

"Well, I'm going out for a smoke then," said Margaret as she headed toward the back where her jacket was hung.

"Not so fast, Margaret." Dylan verbally stopped her. "I've also been instructed not to let anyone outside." The room was quick to fill with moans, groans and disapproving grumbles.

"Why not?" asked Samantha who mostly worked the drive-through.

"I wasn't told that, but he said it was for our safety." Dylan carried on, "I know most of you are upset, but keep in mind, you are on the clock right now and you are getting paid. All you have to do is stay inside. I'm sure most of you have games on your phones you can play or significant others to talk to, so go ahead and do that. Some of you look like you could use a nap—we have plenty of booths you can lie down in. Seems like a pretty sweet deal to me."

The staff appeared to be aligned in agreement as they took his words into consideration. They happily chatted amongst each other as they began to disperse in different directions.

Dylan was about to go back to the office when Michelle spoke up.

"Are we in danger?" she asked. Dylan turned around.

"The thing about that is I'm not sure. I want to say that we're not, and I want that to be true"—Dylan paused—"but I don't think it is. I think there's something terrible afoot."

Michelle felt the same way, and knew she wasn't going to get any decent answers from Dylan, so she walked away to find a cozy place to hide.

Frank had been seated in the Chicken Shack parking lot for well over two hours. He was waiting for them to open; he needed to talk to someone. The sign on the door said they opened at 11:00; however, he hadn't seen anyone come unlock the door, turn on the flashing lights of the Open sign, or flip over the one that said "Closed." He had time to wait, so that's what he did. Music flowed softly from the speakers as the radio played whichever songs the DJ desired. As he sat, staring at the door, waiting for something to happen, another vehicle appeared in the distance. He turned his head to see a car approaching; it didn't appear to be taking its time. It slowed down as it turned into the parking lot, and then sped up again. It came to a screeching halt when it pulled up next to the Bronco. The driver shifted the car into park, killed the engine and got out in a matter of milliseconds. He was dressed as a casual businessman. "Ted" was written on his name tag underneath the heading, "General Manager." He ran to the door on the passenger side of Frank's Bronco and yanked on the handle, only to discover that it was locked.

"Let me in," he demanded, while banging on the window. Frank didn't recognize him, but Frank was here to talk to someone, and this man looked more than eager to do so. Frank pushed the button to unlock the doors and they unlocked. The door swung open. When it closed moments later, Ted was inside.

"What are you doing here?" Ted asked.

"I'm hungry," Frank was slow to reply.

"Bullshit," Ted said. "Why don't you tell me what's really going on?"

"Well . . ." Frank thought for a moment. "It's something terrible, Ted. So now I need to find some answers, and I believe this is the place where I'm going to find 'em."

"Nonsense," Ted declared. "There ain't nothing to find here."

"Are you sure about that?"

"As sure as a whistle."

"That's good," Frank said, nodding his head. "That's good."

"So you'll be on your way now?"

"Yeah." Frank paused. "Yeah, I guess I better get going then."

"Good," Ted said, and let out a sigh of relief. After gathering himself together, he opened the door and stepped out. "Goodbye," he said as he shut the door and walked away. As he made his way toward the restaurant, he realized he didn't hear the Bronco starting up or driving away. Ted turned around. Frank was still there, doing the same thing he had been doing all morning. Sitting and staring. That's when Ted realized his problems wouldn't be going away as peacefully as he'd hoped they would. He marched back to the Bronco, this time approaching the driver's window and instructing Frank to roll it down. Frank obliged.

"What the hell are you doing?" Ted had become clearly irritated. "Why aren't you leaving?"

"Well," Frank said, "I'm still hungry. I think I'd like to get something to eat."

"We're not open."

"Yeah, I saw that, but the sign on the door says you're supposed to be."

"There's been a situation."

"What kind of situation?"

"A none-of-your-business kind of situation."

By this time a majority of the staff inside the Chicken Shack had gathered around the front windows to see what was going on. Michelle suggested calling the cops, but Dylan suggested otherwise.

"That's all right," Frank said, "but I got a situation, too, and the thing about my situation is that it's also your situation."

"Yeah?" Ted spoke heatedly. "How so?"

Frank reached into his pocket and pulled out the feather he had found at the daycare. Ted's face turned pale as he gasped in disbelief. He backed away, returned to the passenger side and got back into Frank's truck, closing the door behind him.

"Where did you get that?" Ted asked.

"I didn't get it, I found it."

"Where? How?"

"In a place it shouldn't have been," Frank answered. "As for the how, that's what I'm trying to find out."

"You think we have something to do with it?"

"With what?

"The missing children," Ted said. "That's why you're here, isn't it? You want to find the children?"

Frank didn't answer. He stared at Ted for a few moments longer, then returned his attention to the feather.

"Where did it come from?" Frank was asking the question.

"Can I look at it?" Ted asked, as he reached his hand toward Frank. Frank pushed the button to lock the doors and handed it over. Ted took the feather and held it up to inspect it under the sunlight. He thought he knew where the feather could have come from, but when he held it under his nose to get a scent, he was certain.

"What can you tell me?" Frank asked.

"That it came from a golden lox chicken," Ted said. "They're a special breed."

"How special?"

"Special enough to be genetically engineered by scientists."

"Why?" Frank asked.

"It's all about the flavour, man. They did it to produce the most perfect-tasting chicken."

"For your restaurant?"

"Yeah," Ted confirmed

"Do you know who's behind it?"

"Harold Earp."

"Isn't he dead?" Frank asked

"That's right, but it doesn't matter, because once the chickens were created, all that was left to do was breed them."

"Who does that?" Frank asked.

"Phil Earp, Harold's great-grandson. He breeds them about seven miles north of town, at the old Calahoo Hills Farm."

"I know where that is."

"Look," Ted said. "Whatever it is that happened, or whatever it is that you find, just know I had nothing to do with it."

"But you know about it?" Frank questioned him.

"I know something's not right. I don't know what it is, though."

"I need the feather back," Frank said. "I gotta go."

Ted was struck with relief when he heard Frank speak those words. He wanted nothing more than for him to leave. Without hesitation he reached across to give back the feather. Frank was about to accept it when he noticed a bandage had been tightly wrapped around Ted's hand.

"What happened to your hand?" Frank asked.

"My hand?" Ted grew nervous. "Nothing. It's . . . it's nothing."

Frank reached behind Ted's head and smashed his face into the dashboard. Ted let the feather float to the ground. Both of his hands were busy applying pressure to the freshness of his broken nose.

"What did you do that for?" Ted choked out, as he spoke through the blood gushing from his nose and trickling down his throat.

"Take it off!" Frank demanded

"Take what off?" Ted cried.

"Your bandage, take it off." Frank was yelling now.

"I can't take it off!"

Frank reached in his coat, pulled out his gun and pressed it tight against Ted's temple.

"You either take the bandage off, or I take your head off."

Ted was hesitant to abide, but the pistol was very convincing. Nervously, he began unwrapping the bandage. Frank held a deadly stare as Ted began to sweat, shaking in fear. Frank was quick to grow impatient. Grabbing a piece of the dangling bandage, he tugged and ripped the whole thing off. Ted screamed and held his hand in pain.

"Show it to me!" Frank shouted.

"It hurts!" Ted cried.

"You want me to relieve it for you?" Frank asked, pressing the pistol harder into his skull.

Ted took a deep breath and held it. Slowly, he let it out, releasing his hand in the process, and showed it to Frank. Ted found himself in a barrel of fear as Frank rekindled his relationship with rage. There, encrusted in Ted's hand, was a scabbed-up hole similar to the size of a kitchen knife. It was surrounded with electrical scars. Fresh blood seeped out the corners of the scabs. They broke open when Frank tore off the bandage.

"I didn't know," Ted cried.

"Didn't know what?"

"I didn't know we were taking the kids! I didn't think the children would be in danger. Not at all. That part was never told to me. I didn't even know they would be there."

Frank listened to the man talk and grew disgusted. He knew that soon he would be stuck listening to him begging for his pathetic life. He stayed silent and let Ted talk.

"What do you want? Anything I can help you with, anything I can do for you," Ted pleaded. "Whatever you want from me, you can have it."

"Your life," Frank said.

"My what?" Ted asked as he felt himself make a mess in his pants.

"Your life," Frank repeated, as they both looked into each other's eyes.

From inside the Chicken Shack the staff couldn't see much of what was happening inside the Bronco. They didn't see when Ted got his face smashed into the dashboard; they never saw the gun the whole time Frank had it held up to Ted's head. But when blood splashed against the windows and glass shattered onto the pavement, they saw it. Then they knew something was wrong; they knew something was very wrong. Michelle was the first to scream, breaking the silence after the shock. Dylan was too ashamed to admit his regret at not calling the cops when Michelle suggested it. If he had listened, Ted would probably still be alive. Feeling the weight of guilt on his shoulders, he ran to the office and got on the phone to call the police. A call that was no longer necessary, for the witnessing staff were already making calls of their own.

Frank reached over Ted's lifeless body and opened the door. He pushed Ted over and used his foot to kick him the rest of the way out. Ted fell flat on the pavement where he continued to bleed out. Frank didn't like the way it sounded, but he was glad that it happened. He started up the Bronco and threw it in reverse. The front tire rolled over Ted's legs as it bounced backwards. He then slammed the brake, causing the passenger door to slam shut. Putting the truck into Drive, he ripped out of the parking lot and headed north. As the sound of his engine faded out, police sirens began to fade in.

Phil was harvesting crops and singing songs of the old days when he heard a vehicle coming. He checked his watch; it was too early for any company he could be expecting, but it wasn't uncommon for folks to just drop in. Sometimes he would even get tourists, people from faraway lands who wanted to see what it was like on Alberta farms. And what better place to do that than the farm on Calahoo Hill? He put his task on hold and headed toward the house to see who it was and what they wanted. He was working in the back and unable to see the driveway from his angle. When he reached the house and went around the corner, he saw a white Ford Bronco parked there. He didn't recognize the vehicle, or know whose blood was splashed inside it, but he did recognize the man standing outside. Phil wasn't a fan of trouble, but dealing with it his whole life, he knew how to handle it. He was good at it. Putting on his best gentleman's smile, he continued heading forward to greet his guest.

"Hello, Frank!" Phil cheerfully shouted out as he moved closer.

"How do you know who I am?" Frank asked.

"Are you kidding me?" Phil asked. "Everybody knows who you are. You've only been blasted on the news twenty-four seven for the past two weeks! They never mentioned anything about you waking up, though." Phil took a moment to analyze Frank.

"Yeah, well it was sudden," Frank explained.

"I reckon it was. Must've been from all those people praying for you."

"Do you know why I'm here?" Frank asked.

"I got a pretty good idea, and if it is what I'm thinking, you'll see there's nothing out here to find," said Phil.

"Then you had better tell me where I can find it," Frank demanded. This made Phil laugh.

"Yeah, and what if I don't?"

"Then you can go hang out with your buddy Ted," Frank said, as he pulled out his pistol. Phil chuckled.

"Ha!" Phil seemed amused. "You planning on shooting me, boy?"

"Not planning on it, but it don't make no difference if I do," Frank stated.

"What do you want? You want to know where the kids are?" Phil asked. "You think I can you tell that? You think I even know?"

"You know something," Frank accused.

"I know they're safe. I know they're alive. I know they're well and taken care of."

"How the hell do you know that?" Frank asked as he became irritated with the weasel of a man.

"How do I know?" Phil repeated the question, which brought him to laughter once again. He had more to say about it, but police sirens could be heard growing in the distance. So he changed the topic. "Oooh, that doesn't sound good," Phill continued. "I wonder what they're going to think when they see that bloody Bronco as they pass by?"

Frank held the gun steady in Phil's face.

"Well, get it over with. Shoot me." Frank didn't move as Phil stood still. "Come on!" Phil yelled. "Be a man, pull the trigger. Shoot me!" Phil's smile faded as he stared into Frank's eyes.

"Don't for one second think I won't." Frank finally spoke.

"I don't, but understand that if you do, you don't get to know what I know. And trust me, I know exactly what you want to know." Phil's smile came back, bringing a few giggles along with it. "Do you want to know who watches over them? Who takes care of them? Who makes sure they get fed?"

Frank remained silent with the gun steadily pointed in Phil's face.

"I do," Phil continued. "I take care of them. You shoot me and I die, then nobody gets to know where they are. And you know what happens then? They starve, Frank. They starve all the way to death."

Phil's voice had been making Frank nauseous, but when he heard the words they carried, his blood boiled. All he had to do was squeeze the trigger and it would all be over. But it wouldn't be over. Phil was right: the kids would still be gone, and that was the only thing he cared about. He was still deciding whether or not to squeeze the trigger, when he noticed the sirens had made themselves a lot louder.

"Uh-oh," Phil spoke tauntingly. "That don't sound good. Maybe we oughta hide your truck." Frank didn't have to think much longer about making a decision, mostly because he didn't have the time for it. Frank lowered his gun. Phil's grin widened. "Come on," he said as he walked away. "You can bring it to the back and hide it in the barn." He went to the passenger side of the Bronco and hopped in. Frank watched in bewilderment as Phil made himself comfortable in the bloody mess.

"What are you waiting for? We ain't got all day," Phil shouted at Frank through the window when he noticed he hadn't moved. Frank knew Phil was right, as the sirens were even louder now. He ran to the Bronco and got in. Starting it up, he drove behind the house and toward the barn, following Phil's directions.

The door to the barn was already open, which made it easy for Frank to just drive inside. He killed the engine and they both got out. Phil ran back toward the entrance.

"I'll shut this so they won't see inside if they decide to get nosy. You just wait in here," Phil said. Frank didn't trust anything about it.

"I'll wait outside," Frank said, as he ran to keep up with Phil to avoid getting locked in.

"They might see you," Phil warned convincingly.

"I'll take my chances." Frank spoke so sternly that Phil saw no reason to argue. Frank stepped out and began creeping around to the far side of the barn, away from the road. Phil pushed the door shut and headed toward the house. The sirens were firing at full blast as the police cars went speeding past. Four cruisers went by, and not one of them stopped or even slowed down. Phil could be seen from the road as they drove past; Frank and his Bronco remained out of sight. Then, as quickly as the sirens came to be, they faded away.

Frank stepped back out from his hiding place and into the open. He wasn't done with Phil, not yet. Frank was set to get some answers. He made a beeline across the field in Phil's direction. Phil looked over and saw him coming. It was no surprise; he knew he would be coming. He began walking toward Frank, as well, in order to do the kindness of meeting him half way.

"Where are the kids?" Frank shouted as he neared. Phil didn't answer, he just smiled as he had been doing all along. Frank realized he was dealing with a madman; Phil failed to realize he was dealing with one, as well. When they were within arm's reach, Frank grabbed Phil by the throat lifting him high into the air. Phil coughed and choked as he kicked helplessly, struggling for breath. Frank tightened his grasp and pulled him in for a face-to-face confrontation. Unfortunately, Frank pulled him in too close and Phil's foot was able to make generous contact with his nuts. Frank lost his grip as Phil tumbled to the ground, gasping for air. He rolled away and scrambled forward in an attempt to put some distance between them. Frank had fallen over and was on the ground, as well, feeling a pain that no man was ever meant to feel. By the time he could pick himself up,

Phil had run all the way around to the front of the house. Frank wasn't sure if he was taking off or going inside. He assumed the latter. He figured Phil had become frightened and ran to lock himself out of harm's way. He had no concerns about him calling the cops. He knew Phil had something to hide—that's why he helped hide Frank and the Bronco; he didn't want the cops poking around.

Frank was now facing the back of the house. He decided his best move was to go check inside. He walked forward with the intention of entering the rear. When he got within reaching distance, he extended his arm to pull open the door. Instead, the door flung open on its own, sending Frank flying to the ground. He looked up to see Phil strolling out with his signature grin and a twelve-gauge shotgun. He took aim at Frank, but Frank didn't beg for mercy like Phil thought he would. Frank was prepared to die and willing to do it if he had to; he was willing to do it for the kids. Phil realized this, and recognized Frank as a risk not worth taking. Frank looked up into Phil's eyes and understood his mind was made up. He closed his eyes and waited. Phil squeezed the trigger.

"Shit," Phil said as the gun merely clicked. He took some necessary steps back to place some distance between him and Frank.

When Frank opened his eyes, he saw Phil frantically fishing through his pockets. It had become apparent he was looking for shotgun shells. Frank understood that Phil failed to load the gun and was quick to spring back to his feet. Phil had found a couple of bullets and was fumbling to get them loaded. Frank grabbed the barrel to snatch it away, but Phil pulled back, dropping the bullets in the process. Frank's grip wasn't firm enough, and the gun slipped out of his grasp. Phil took a step back, swinging the gun down around and up into Frank's chin. Frank's whole body jerked up as he got rocked, leaving him knocked out in the grass.

Phil reached down and picked up the fallen shotgun shells. Opening the chamber, he slid them in.

"It's quite the mess you got yourself into, boy," Phil said as he raised the surely loaded weapon and took aim at Frank. "Yes, quite the mess," Phil repeated to himself, speaking beneath his breath. "Quite the mess." He was thinking deep thoughts. Blowing Frank's head off would create quite a mess, and with the cops roaming around, it didn't seem wise to do something so bold. He began to drag him toward the house so he could get him to the basement. Since he was there, there was something he wanted to show him. Then he would kill him. As he dragged him across the lawn, the bumps in the ground bounced Frank around enough to conjure his consciousness. Phil noticed and thought maybe he would have to kill him out here after all. But not before he got the chance to show him what he wanted to show him. Phil released Frank's leg and punched him hard in the face to keep him weak. Frank, unable to move well, simply took the blow. He was weak, but he was alert. Phil took him to the side of the house and dropped him by the basement window. Grabbing Frank by the back of the head, he pressed his face against the glass.

"You see that?" Phil chuckled at Frank. "Do you see?" Frank looked, and he did see.

"That's how close you came." Phil laughed at him. "That's how close you came to saving them."

Frank began to wonder when Phil would finally kill him. He wondered what it would feel like; he wondered what it would sound like. He listened, waiting to hear the gun blast. Instead he heard sirens. It was the police again. There must have been some kind of trouble in town, because they were on their way back, and they were on their way in a hurry.

Phil released Frank's head and it dropped like a sack of bricks. Frank was out of it, but he wasn't out. So once again, making use of the butt of his gun, Phil smashed Frank in the back of the head, initiating nap time.

The sirens were getting louder as they drew near. Phil's focus was on getting Frank out of sight. He set the gun down where they stood so he could use all of his leverage and strength to get Frank inside as quickly and efficiently as possible. It wasn't hard for Phil to drag him; he got him inside and out of sight without any issues. He hauled Frank across the floor to the door that stood directly ahead when entering. He opened it up to reveal a set of descending stairs. He got Frank to the edge of the steps and gave him a shove. It made Phil laugh, seeing the way he tumbled down. After coming to a sudden stop, Frank lay motionless at the bottom. Phil ran down and knelt over him to examine his condition.

"Wake up," Phil said, as he gave his face a good slap. "You're gonna want to see this."

Frank began to stir. Phil grabbed his arm and continued to drag him farther along. They reached a second door, this one with a padlock holding it shut. Phil released Frank's arm, reached into his pocket and pulled out a key. Frank lay mildly awake as Phill unlocked it. Removing the lock and unlatching the hook, he reached back into his pocket to reveal another key. This one he used to unlock the lock in the handle. Then, twisting the knob and giving a push, he opened it up.

"Have a look, Frank," Phil said as he picked up Frank's head, adjusting it so he could see inside. Frank's vision was blurry but he could see them—he could see them all. Even the missing staff. They were all alive, but they weren't all well. Sitting in rows at tables with their heads down and their hands sewing. Every expression on every face in the room was one of doom and gloom. Frank wondered what had happened to get them to act this way, what Phil had done to commit them to such obedience. At first, Frank thought they were making toys. The place was designed in such a way to resemble Santa's workshop. As his focus got clearer, he understood it wasn't toys they were making, but shoes they were sewing.

"Well," Phil asked, "what do you think?"

"I think you're sick," Frank said. Phil laughed.

"They're nice, though," Phil continued. "The shoes . . . am I right?" It took Frank a moment to understand what he was talking about. Then he remembered the shoes he himself had been wearing. He looked at his feet, then back at the children's creations. They were the same.

"You're a bad man," Frank stated. "Get those darn things off me." Frank began trying to slip his sneakers off with his feet.

"Come on now." Phil smiled. "Don't be getting nasty with me."

"Why?" Frank asked. "Why are you doing this?"

"Why do you think, Frank?" Phil asked the question instead. Frank couldn't think of a possible reason, so he made no response. "There was money involved," Phil said as he leaned in. "How could I not?"

"Why them, though? Why can't you make them yourself?"

"That is a great question, Frank, and I just happen to have the answer for you. These deluxe luxury shoes were engineered at the exact same super lab we got our chickens from. A very precise design that no machine is capable of creating. No grown fingers are small enough to do the stitching."

"I understand that, but I don't understand how stealing children ever came to be an option." Phil gave Frank a stiff slap in the face. He didn't appreciate the accusation.

"I didn't steal them," Phil said. "What kind of scum do you think I am?"

"Then tell me how they got here," Frank demanded.

"I bought them, Frank, fair and square. I own them."

"What do you mean own them?"

"Come on, Frank. I can't believe I'm explaining this to you." Phil spoke with honest disbelief. "Listen, a daycare is a secure place, a very secure place. You think Ted and I could have just waltzed in there on our own?"

"That wasn't a waltz you two performed—you smashed through the darn window," Frank accused.

"But don't you think a broken window would have set off an alarm?"

Frank thought about it and knew Phil was right. When the window broke, security should have been alerted, the alarm should have been blaring, help should have been coming. None of that happened, but why? As soon as Frank came up with that question, he was able to think of an answer. The security system had been shut off. Most of the staff had a code to disarm it, but not many had access to disable the system completely. As far as Frank knew, there was only one person who could. Coincidentally, that person had made claims to having lots of money. Coincidentally, that person had been looking to run away.

"What about the kids, Frank?" Phil asked. "How do you think they slept through all of it? Lullabies won't make them sleep that well." Phil paused for a moment, and then his face lit up with dramatic effect. "But Ketamine will."

"But who?" Frank asked. "And when?"

"It was in the juice—Patricia mixed it in the night before. All we had to do after that was wait for it to be served, which you did quite well if I don't say so myself." Phil let out a cruel laugh. "Do you get it now?" he asked, as he continued to giggle. He could see in Frank's face that he understood.

"How long do you think you could possibly keep this up?" Frank asked.

"As long as I goddamn want." Phil spoke with authority. Frank looked up at him with eyes of fury. Phil didn't like it and he ditched his smile. "I can see you plan on continuing to be a problem. I wish I hadn't left my gun outside, boy. I'd blow a hole in you so big that a tyrannosaurus dick wouldn't be able to stretch it any further."

Frank began to fill with rage. His fists were clenched and ready to fly, as he felt his energy making a grand comeback. Phil felt Frank's strength recovering, and began to panic. Knowing he could never outmatch Frank, he released his head while pushing it into the corner of the doorway. When Frank's head made contact with the door frame, rather than causing further injury, it made him more alert, more aware. Frank picked himself off the ground and stood to face his enemy. The Life and Times of Farmer Phil was about to reach a stunning conclusion.

Phil took a couple of steps back and planted himself where he wished to stand his ground. Frank was eager to attack, but wise to be patient, for Phil had a sleeve full of trickery.

"What's the matter, Frank?" Phil asked tauntingly. "Are you scared?"

"No, scared isn't the word," Frank said. "I'm just trying to figure out what trick you got up your sleeve."

"Don't be silly, Frank. These sleeves aren't big enough to hold tricks," Phil said as he rolled them up to prove a point.

When Frank felt comfortable enough to take a step forward, Phil took a step back, reaching into his pocket and pulling out a revolver.

"Gosh darn you," Frank growled through gritted teeth.

"Any last words?"

Before Frank and Phil ended up inside the house, prior to Frank being shown the kids through the basement window, Lieutenants Daniels and Richinski were on their way back into town. They had been headed up north with three other cruisers when they caught a tip that a white Ford Bronco had been seen headed in that direction. When they weren't catching up to any vehicles of interest, they thought it would be best to turn back and thoroughly investigate the area they left behind them. Daniels watched from the passenger seat as Richinski drove, with the sirens still blaring.

"You think maybe we should shut those off?" asked Daniels. "All they're gonna do is keep him in hiding."

Richinski had forgotten they were even on. It was a sound he'd become accustomed to over the years. He shut them off without saying anything about it, feeling slightly foolish for having left them on in the first place. As they drove on, Calahoo Hills Farm appeared on the horizon.

"Should we check over there?" Richinski asked. "See if he's seen anything? I saw him standing outside earlier when we passed by." They sat in silence for a moment as Daniels thought about it.

"No," Daniels said. "I don't think it'd be worth our while. You know how Phil feels about the law."

"I know he doesn't like it."

"I don't see us getting any cooperation out of him. It'd end up to be nothing but a headache."

"But what if Frank's there?" Richinski mentioned the possibility.

"Then he's there," Daniels said as they moved along.

The farm was on the right side of the road as they headed toward town. Richinski paid attention to driving, while Daniels looked out for anything suspicious. He paid more attention to the farm when they got closer. He thought about what Richinski had said and wondered if passing the place by was the right thing to do. Phil was a hothead, and he'd had several—if not dozens—of altercations with the police, none of them even remotely friendly. Everything looked normal out there, anyway. It was quiet; there didn't seem to be anyone around.

He caught sight of the front porch. The main door to the house was left open; the screen door in front of it was shut. Everything appeared to be tidy and in order. Vehicles and farm equipment were lined up neatly beside the garage. Crops sprouting in perfect rows. Chickens and cows looking nurtured and fed. A well-maintained lawn . . . and a shotgun on the ground by the side of the house.

"Stop the car," Daniels ordered.

"What's the matter?" Richinski asked as he slowed down to a halt.

"Back up," Daniels demanded. "We're going to the farm."

"What changed your mind?"

"Why don't you look over there and see for yourself?" Daniels pointed behind them. When Richinski turned to look, he spotted the gun instantly.

"I'll be damned," Richinski said to himself. "Should I call it in?"

"And have a bunch of rookies muck it up?" Daniels asked. "No, let's check it out ourselves first."

Richinski put the car in reverse, slowly backing up to the farm's driveway. After pulling in, they waited a moment to see if anyone would come out. When nobody did, they exited the vehicle. Daniels noticed fresh tire tracks going further along up the dirt road and toward the barn. He took a mental note, and headed up to the house to investigate the gun. Once they reached it, Richinski knelt down for a closer examination.

"Look." Richinski pointed to the butt of it.

"Fresh blood," Daniels said, confirming he saw what Richinski was seeing. Daniels got a bad feeling in his gut but chose to ignore it, turning his attention to the barn.

"I think we should check out the barn," Daniels suggested.

"What about the house?" Richinski asked.

"If Phil is home, he might not let us in, and then we would have to leave. We should use this opportunity to have a look around. See as much as we can before he has a chance to kick us off his property."

"Why the barn, though?" Richinski wondered. "Am I missing something?"

"Fresh tracks," Daniels replied. "I saw them when we got out. They lead up there." Richinski looked at the barn, then toward the ground to see the tracks that his partner was talking about.

Daniels began heading toward the barn. Richinski looked back at the house, wondering what was the right thing to do. He wasn't sure, but he knew it was the wrong thing to argue with Daniels. He picked up the gun and brought it along as he followed him out to the barn. They were cautiously quiet as they made their approach. The barn door was slightly ajar. Daniels reached his fingers in and pulled it open.

Richinski's jaw dropped. Daniels wasn't fazed; he had been around long enough to get used to surprises. There, before them, was the vehicle they had been searching for. The great white Ford Bronco, as described by the Chicken Shack staff.

"I think it's time we check out that house," Daniels said.

Richinski was already on board. Picking up their pace, they walked with purpose toward the house and unholstered their service pistols. Time seemed to slow as they made their approach. The wind was all that could be heard; not even the crickets dared to make a sound.

Daniels was the first to notice the condition of the back door. Clearly there had been some type of altercation. The door had been left open, so they carefully stepped up to have a look inside.

"Is anybody home?" Daniels shouted. He was left without a reply. Motioning for Richinski to follow, he stepped inside.

There wasn't much that seemed out of the ordinary. Richinski was feeling quite certain that no one was home. That was until they heard the noises coming from the basement. The two officers cautiously made their way toward the stairs and began their descent. As they crept down the steps, the sounds became more audible. It was voices; there was an argument taking place. Both Daniels and Richinski knew it wasn't going to end well. The creaks went unnoticed as they slowly made their descent, one step at a time. When they got to the bottom, Daniels continued to take the lead and poked his head around the corner. Two men were engaged in a heated conversation. One, he recognized to be Frank; the other he knew as Phil, who had just removed a revolver from his pocket as he was fixing to take aim.

"Freeze!" Daniels shouted as he pointed his gun at Phil.

Phil reacted before he had the chance to think. Turning around, he fired two shots. Both of them struck Daniels. The first one hit his shoulder, and the pain from the bullet ripping through made him drop his gun. The second bullet hit his head, and all the pain went away.

Richinski sank into a pit of disbelief as he looked down at his recently deceased partner.

"Hold on," Phil said to Richinski as he dropped his gun, realizing he had just killed a cop. "This is trespassing, isn't it?"

Richinski was still looking at his partner.

"It is," Phil continued. "I'm right. No one invited you in, this is private property . . . I'm in the clear, right?" Phil spoke with desperation.

Richinski finally regained focus, as Phil came to the realization that there was no way to sugar-coat the situation. He'd killed a cop; he knew he would end up serving some time, he just wasn't sure how much of it. Ready to surrender, Phil put his hands in the air and dropped to his knees.

The first shot startled Frank. It was the only one Phil felt as it tore through his chest and dropped him all the way to the ground. Richinski held his aim on him and fired four more times. Frank looked on with pleasure as he watched the stains grow on Phil's shirt as he bled out. When Frank lifted his eyes back up, Richinski's aim was now turned on him.

"Get your hands up," Richinski demanded. Frank obliged. "Slowly step toward me."

"The kids are here," Frank said as he began stepping forward.

"What kids?" Richinski asked.

"The ones that were kidnapped from the daycare. They're in that room." Frank motioned to the door behind him.

"Are you serious?" Richinski said. "All of them?"

"I think so, at least most of them."

Richinski cautiously came toward Frank and peeked through the door. Frank was right, they were in there.

"What the heck is going on here, Frank?" Richinski spoke softly as the question was more for himself.

"Whatever it is, it's not over."

"For you it is," Richinski stated. "The entire staff working at the Chicken Shack witnessed you murder their manager."

"He was involved," Frank explained. "He deserved to die, just like Phil, and just like Patricia."

"Patricia?"

"She's the owner of the daycare," Frank explained. "She was the one who set it all up. I don't know how much she got, but it must have been a lot."

"What do you mean?" Richinski said. "I'm confused."

"What, are you blind?" Frank asked him. "Can't you see? They paid her. They paid her to look the other way. They weren't intruders, they were guests. They were invited, welcomed in to take whatever they pleased, so they did."

"This Patricia," Richinski was asking. "Does she have a last name?"

"She did," Frank replied. "It's most likely changed by now."

"And what proof do you have?" Richinski asked.

"Proof?" Frank said. "I don't believe I got any proof."

"Then it doesn't matter."

"It doesn't matter?" Frank responded with a hint of anger. "What about the children? Don't they matter?"

"Of course they matter, and we will launch a thorough investigation. If the woman formerly known as Patricia is involved, trust me, we will find out."

"Yeah, when it's too late. She'll be long gone by the time you link her to the case."

"The law has a long arm."

"Well, it wasn't long enough to stop that bullet from ripping through your partner, now was it?" Richinski looked behind him at the foot of the stairs where Daniels lay in silence.

"Listen," Frank continued. "Even if you do find her, what's going to happen? She goes to trial, gets a good lawyer, 'cause you know she has the money for it. Most likely, he gets her off completely. The odds aren't against that outcome and you know it, but even if they were, and even if she was found guilty, what's the worst that could happen? Huh? What's the worst they're going to do to her? And let's say the judge does decide to throw the book at her, what's she looking at? Three, maybe three-and-a-half years? She'd be out on the streets again in nine months with good behaviour, and last time I checked she didn't even know the definition of acting up. You know darn well that justice will be on vacation the day her verdict is read, just like it takes a vacation on all the other child abductors and abusers in the Canadian justice system. I'm no psychic, but logically thinking, as it stands, she either gets away clean, or suffers a foam-fingered slap on a padded wrist. I know these children went through hell, as did their parents. You don't believe me, poke your head in there again and look at their faces. Those aren't the faces of children, they've aged. Life for them isn't fun anymore, and for some of them, it never will be again. Imagine being four years old and having already lived the best day of your life. Patricia needs to get what she deserves."

"What does she deserve?" Richinski asked.

"Well, your partner's dead, isn't he? Maybe we should start there."

"Are you suggesting she deserves to die?"

"I'm not suggesting." Frank spoke sincerely. "It's what I'm telling you. My suggestion is toward something else."

"Well, what the heck is it?"

"Let me do it," Frank said. "I can find her a lot quicker than you guys, not because you can't, but because you have to follow rules. I don't. Just like you don't have to keep me here."

"I gotta stop you there," Richinski interrupted.

"No, you don't," Frank continued, ignoring the interruption. "Listen, if you don't want me to do it for the children, that's fine. If you don't want me to do it for their parents, well that's fine too. But if I can't do it for them, then let me do it for him." Frank pointed toward Daniels. "Does your partner not deserve justice?"

Richinski was slow to respond. He was thinking long and hard about it. It shocked him when he realized he was actually thinking about letting him do it.

"You know I can't do that, Frank," Richinski finally replied. "A fistful of crimes have been committed by your hands. You need to answer to the law just like anybody else."

"I'll come back," Frank said

"You'll what?" asked Richinski

"You heard what I said." After Frank spoke these words, Richinski began to lower his gun. He was really taking this into consideration.

"How do I know you're telling the truth?" Richinski asked.

"You don't," said Frank with pure determination in his eyes. Richinski holstered his gun.

"I'm going up to the cruiser to call this in. You got five minutes to get out of here. I don't know which way you're going and neither will they." Richinski paused. "You do what needs to get done. In forty-eight hours or less, I want to get a phone call from you, and I want you to tell me that you're on Hamburger Hill. You know where that is?"

"Yeah," Frank said as he nodded his head.

"All right, I want you to tell me that you're on Hamburger Hill, because I want you to be on Hamburger Hill. Then I'll come get you. You understand?"

"Yes, Lieutenant," said Frank. "Thank you, Lieutenant."

"You got five minutes, Frank," Richinski said. "Get the heck out of here."

Frank ran past Richinski with haste, hopped over Daniels and went up the stairs. Richinski watched him and couldn't help but smile. Yes, it was a bad situation, but for the first time in a long time, justice would be served: a real, truthful justice. It was what the children deserved. He began his trek up the stairs. By the time he got to the top and out to the cruiser, Frank was long gone.

Later when the crew arrived they would find out the Bronco had been left behind. It was then that Richinski noticed a gap in the row of vehicles alongside the farming equipment. Frank had acquired a new vehicle, but with Phil dead, they had no way of knowing what kind of vehicle it was. Richinski wasn't concerned; he knew in forty-eight hours this whole situation would be behind him. It wasn't long before the parents began showing up and running onto the scene, looking to be reunited with the ones they thought were gone forever. Tears of joy were on everyone's faces. Richinski was thinking about the death of his partner. He paid the price so those kids could be saved; if Daniels had known what was going to happen, he still would have done the same thing. He would have thought it was worth it. He made Richinski proud. A tear slipped out the corner of his eye. Whether it was a tear of joy or a tear of sadness is unknown.

* * * * * * * * *

On a not-so tropical beach in Alberta, Canada, Felicity Coombs lay on her back on the sun-soaked sand. Felicity was her new name, because she was a new person. She just needed to get to a new place, a faraway place. In the meantime she would be in hiding. The Alberta beach wasn't exactly popular, which was why it was so dead that day. She had found an isolated location farther down the shore where no one really went. Needless to say, she had the beach to herself, as she lay in the sand, under the setting sun.

She tried to relax, but she was quite nervous. In the beginning, she never even thought about getting caught, but as time passed, and guilt got the chance to marinate itself in her soul, she thought about it a lot. She closed her eyes and began thinking about other things, anything, just not the one thing. She wondered why she ever even did it, but once she remembered, she was able to convince herself to think happy thoughts. She did it for the money, she did it for a brand-new life with a brand-new start. She began to smile as she thought about the fancy life awaiting her.

When the blissful silence of the afternoon was disturbed by a large splashing sound, Felicity bolted up, returning to her nervous state. Glancing across the beach, she saw nothing but bare sand and open water. It was probably just a fish popping up to catch some bugs, she thought.

"Come on, Patricia, quit being so paranoid," she said to herself, forgetting that she had a new name.

Before long she was back to fantasizing about her future and how fancy it was going to be. That's when she heard the noise again. This time it wasn't a splash, but a voice. A voice she recognized all too well.

"Hello, Patricia." It was Frank. She opened her eyes, and as quick as a rabbit, she was on her feet, wishing she hadn't been so dismissive earlier.

"Frank!" Fear was in her voice. "What are you doing here?"

"You know darn well." Frank spoke with aggression. "What's the matter? You didn't think I would find out?"

"No," she admitted, "I always knew you would."

"You didn't think I would find you?" he asked.

"No," she replied, "I knew you could do that too. I just didn't think you would be alive long enough for it to happen."

"A lot of lives have been ruined because of you, because of what you did." Frank paused to give her a chance to speak. It was a chance she didn't take advantage of.

Frank continued. "Remember when you told me to kill them all?" Frank waited for a reply and she only nodded her head. "You didn't want them dead because of what they did, you wanted them dead because of what they knew."

"Why—why are you here?" She finally broke her silence. "Why you? Where are the cops?"

"Out writing tickets and chasing bad guys."

"So why aren't they here?" she asked. "Why aren't they out here arresting me?" Once she realized, she began to speak with the confidence of someone who thought they'd gotten away with a crime. "They don't know I did anything—they got nothing on me." She paused to look at Frank and her smile returned. "But they got something on you, don't they, Frank?" She felt like she had the upper hand. "The whole world knows about what you did at the Chicken Shack." Frank remained silent; it was his turn to listen. "So what are you here for? Money? Is that what you're after?"

"That's not why I'm here."

"Then why are you?" she asked, without giving him time to respond. "Never mind, I don't care. I think maybe I should just call the cops myself."

"I don't think you'll be able to pull it off," Frank said.

"Oh yeah?" she said. "And why not?"

"Because it'll take you two seconds to pick up your phone, another one-point-eight seconds to unlock it, assuming you do keep it locked, which I believe someone like you would. Another zero-point-seven seconds to get to the dial pad and another point nine to dial nine-one-one. On top of that, you gotta add the five seconds it's going to take for you to think about what I've said once I've finished saying it.

"Now, if you add all that up together, you're going to get ten-point-four seconds. The reason that doesn't work is because you only have five seconds left to be alive." When he was finished speaking, all she could do was stare at him in awe and disbelief, trying to grasp the reality of what he'd said. Once she saw him pulling out his gun, she realized what he meant. Frantically, she began scrambling for her phone.

Frank was the only one who heard the gun blast on the beach that evening. Patricia's fantasies and daydreams were now spread across the beach along with her blood and shattered skull. Frank dropped the gun into the sand. He didn't need it, not anymore. He walked away, leaving her to be discovered later that night, when the coyotes came out.

Five hours and forty-seven kilometres later, Frank found himself at the bottom of Hamburger Hill. Looking up, he admired its beauty. Taking a few steps up, he plopped down on the grass of the slope. He was tired; it had been a helluva day. Pulling his phone out of his pocket, he unlocked it and dialed a number. Holding it up to his ear, he lay down to gaze at the stars. It began to ring.

Back at the police station, Richinski sat at his desk reviewing notes from the events of that twisted day. He was thinking about calling it a night and getting a drink to de-stress, when the phone started ringing. He considered ignoring it, and never really did understand why he didn't.

"Yeah?" Richinski answered. It was all he had the energy to say.

"It's Frank."

Richinski perked up.

"I'm done."